Maurice Sendak's REALLY ROSIE

starring the Nutshell Kids

scenario, lyrics, and pictures by Maurice Sendak

music by Carole King | design by Jane Byers Bierhorst

Harper & Row, Publishers   New York, Evanston, San Francisco, London

FOR FELIX

This book is based on the television program *Maurice Sendak's Really Rosie Starring the Nutshell Kids*, Sheldon Riss, Executive Producer, first televised on the CBS network on February 19, 1975. The program was adapted from *Nutshell Library*, copyright © 1962 by Maurice Sendak, and *The Sign on Rosie's Door*, copyright © 1960 by Maurice Sendak.

The pictures on pages 1, 4, 9, 11, 13, 14 (lower left), 15 (left), 16, 17 (upper left), 18, 19, 23, 25 (lower right), 29, and 31 and the lion sequence in the corner of the right-hand pages are cels from the animated film *Really Rosie*, created by the artists of D & R Productions, Inc., working under the supervision of Ron Fritz and Dan Hunn. Some of the many preliminary drawings that Maurice Sendak made for the guidance of the animators are reproduced on pages 2, 3, 5, 6, 7, 8, 10, 12, 14 (upper left), 15 (right), 17 (lower middle), 21, 22, 24, 25 (upper right), 26, 27, 28, 30, and 32.

CAST OF CHARACTERS

ROSIE   Director, producer, the star of her block | *age ten*
KATHY   Rosie's only girl friend and her opposite in every way | *age eight*

the Nutshell Kids

JOHNNY   Bookish and shy | *age seven*
PIERRE   Negative, violent, and very loud | *age seven*
ALLIGATOR   Cute and desperate to please | *age five*
CHICKEN SOUP   Loves to eat, perform, and most of all, loves Rosie | *age eight*

JENNIE   Johnny's dog
BUTTERMILK   Rosie's cat

various mamas and papas, a lion, a doctor, a tiger, a robber, a blackbird, a rat, a
turtle, and a monkey

SETTING | *A Brooklyn street with typical attached brick houses. The action takes
place on the front steps—the stoop—of Rosie's house, and later in the cellar.
The time is now, from morning to early evening of a hot July day.*

It is early morning. Rosie appears at her window and begins to sing. Kathy, the Nutshell Kids, various mamas and papas, Jennie, and Buttermilk poke their heads out of their windows and listen.

REALLY ROSIE

I'm really Rosie
And I'm Rosie Real.
You better believe me
I'm a great big deal!
BE-LIEVE ME!
(chorus) BE-LIEVE ME!
I'm a star from afar,
Off the golden coast.
Beat that drum! Make that toast!
To Rosie the most!
BE-LIEVE ME!
(chorus) BE-LIEVE ME!
I can sing
"Tea for two and two for tea,"
I can act
"To be or not to be,"

I can tap
across the Tappan Zee.
Hey, can't you see?
I'm terrific at everything!
No star shines so bright as me.
ROSIE!
BE-LIEVE ME!
(chorus) BE-LIEVE ME!

The stoop. Children sitting on the steps. Pierre leaning out of his window.

ROSIE   *(The boys make nasty comments during this speech.)* Yes, my name is Rosie. I am a star. I'm famous and wonderful and everybody loves me and wants to be me. Who can blame them? Now I'm going to make the movie of my life. It will be a very classy movie, mostly about me and those beloved few who helped me up the ladder of success. Johnny. And Alligator. *(snicker)* Pierre! And my darling Chicken Soup. Hey, where is he? Oh well, lover boy is never far from his Rosie—except if he's eating his chicken soup.

JOHNNY   Rosie's starting again.

ALLIGATOR   *(leaning on Johnny)* Who cares.

PIERRE   I don't care!

JOHNNY   *(shoving Alligator away)* Nuts!

ALLIGATOR   *(kicking Johnny's book up in the air)* To you too!

ROSIE   (*sighing*) Well, here we are. Where it all was.

KATHY   What was, Rosie?

ROSIE   *I* was, dummy.

KATHY   Can I be in your real-life movie story, Rosie?

ROSIE   Any experience?

KATHY   I can dance!

ROSIE   Seeing is believing.

(*Kathy does a clumsy, lumbering dance.*)

ROSIE   I don't believe it.

(*The boys, hooting, do a vulgar imitation of Kathy's dance.*)

KATHY   Those stupid boys make me nervous. I can dance like
a dream! (*She sticks her tongue out at the boys.*)

(*Everybody slumps on the stoop again, bored.*)

ALLIGATOR   (*whining*) Where's Chicken Soup?

(*They all seem to think about it.*)

PIERRE   (*mad cackle*) Maybe he fell in his soup and got
drowned! (*makes choking noise*)

(*All look depressed. Except Rosie. We watch an idea dawn
on her.*)

ROSIE   (*very pointedly and casually, to Kathy*) I suppose you're
dying to know the name of my movie?

(*Kathy nods, speechless. The boys try to look disinterested.*)

ROSIE   (*pausing dramatically*) Did You Hear What Happened to
Chicken Soup?

KATHY   What! What! What!

ROSIE   That's the name of my movie: *Did You Hear What Happened to Chicken Soup?* You'll have to wait and see what happened—*and it's all true!*

> (*The boys are hopelessly hooked. They lean forward eagerly, waiting for Rosie to "haul" them in. She smells success and is triumphant.*)

ROSIE   O.K. My movie is about to start!

> (*Everybody struggles to be first on line.*)

ROSIE   (*looking upward*) Hey, Ma! My director's chair!

> (*A window opens and a folding chair drops onto the pavement. Rosie sinks into it luxuriously. The kids are pushing and falling over each other.*)

ROSIE   Easy boys. One at a time. (*eyes Johnny up and down theatrically*)

JOHNNY   Hey, Rosie, so what happened to Chicken Soup?

ROSIE   You'll find out O.K. if I let you act in my picture. First, your screen test. What are you going to do?

JOHNNY   I'll do "One Was Johnny."

ROSIE   Terrific! O.K. Take one!

ONE WAS JOHNNY

1 was Johnny who lived by himself
2 was a rat who jumped on his shelf
3 was a cat who chased the rat
4 was a dog who came in and sat
5 was a turtle who bit the dog's tail
6 was a monkey who brought in the mail
7 a blackbird pecked poor Johnny's nose
8 was a tiger out selling old clothes
9 was a robber who took an old shoe
10 was a puzzle. What should Johnny do?

He stood on a chair and said,
"Here's what I'll do—I'll start
to count backwards
and when I am through—
if this house isn't empty
I'll eat all of you!!!!"

9 was the robber who left looking pale
8 was the tiger who chased him to jail
7 the blackbird flew off to Havana
6 was the monkey who stole a banana
5 was the turtle who crawled off to bed
4 was the dog who slid home on a sled
3 was the cat who pounced on the rat
2 was the rat who left with the cat
1 was Johnny who lived by himself
AND LIKED IT LIKE THAT!

ROSIE   You're terrific, sweetheart. I'll make you a star!

JOHNNY   (*doggedly*) So what happened to Chicken Soup?

ROSIE   (*winks and looks arch*) O.K. gang! Let's get this show on the road!

ALLIGATOR   Hey, Ma!

    (*A bag falls out of a window, narrowly missing him.*
    He throws a suspicious glance upward and then rushes over
    to Rosie.)

ALLIGATOR   Now me, Rosie?

ROSIE   Now me what?

ALLIGATOR   You know, my screen test.

ROSIE   What do you do?

ALLIGATOR   Oh, you know, Rosie.

ROSIE   Yeah, the alphabet. Boring.

ALLIGATOR   I'm terrific!

ROSIE   Uhh huh.

ALLIGATOR   (*starts crying*) Oh please, Rosie!

ROSIE   O.K. O.K. Take one.

ALLIGATORS ALL AROUND

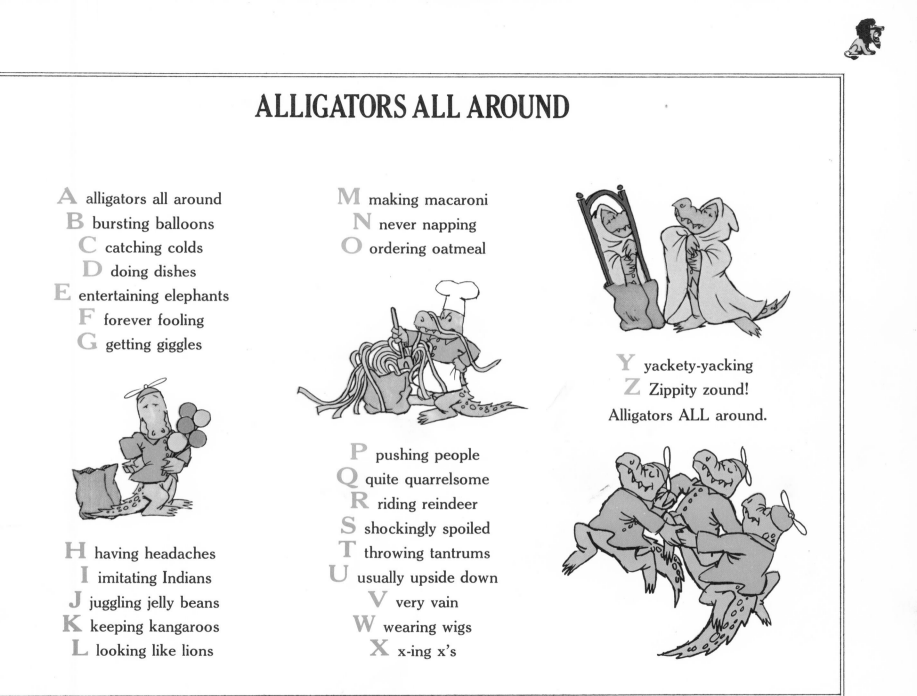

A alligators all around
B bursting balloons
C catching colds
D doing dishes
E entertaining elephants
F forever fooling
G getting giggles

H having headaches
I imitating Indians
J juggling jelly beans
K keeping kangaroos
L looking like lions

M making macaroni
N never napping
O ordering oatmeal

P pushing people
Q quite quarrelsome
R riding reindeer
S shockingly spoiled
T throwing tantrums
U usually upside down
V very vain
W wearing wigs
X x-ing x's

Y yackety-yacking
Z Zippity zound!
Alligators ALL around.

ROSIE   That's real cute, but don't call us, we'll call you. (*Rosie points to Pierre in his window.*)

PIERRE   Don't start on me, Rosie! I don't care what happened to Chicken Soup!

ROSIE   It's a pity you won't be in my life story.

PIERRE   I don't care about your life story! And I don't care what happened to Chicken Soup! And anyway, nothing happened.

ROSIE   Nothing happened? You gotta be kidding! It was so horrible! Uuch! If only he hadn't been eat—

PIERRE   He was eaten? Who ate him?

   (*All the kids look and wait breathlessly.*)

ROSIE   What suffering! I'm not lyin', I—

PIERRE   A lion! A lion ate him!!! (*Rosie smiles knowingly. Pierre is ecstatic.*) I know what happened to Chicken Soup! It's the story of my life!

ROSIE   Really? Let's see.

   (*All are caught up in the excitement of Pierre's impending performance.*)

PIERRE   (*screaming hoarsely*) O.K. Here I COME!

ROSIE   (*sotto voce*) Lights! Action! Camera!

PIERRE

PROLOGUE

There once was a boy named Pierre
who only would say,
"I don't care!"
Read his story, my friend,
for you'll find at the end
that a suitable moral lies there.

CHAPTER 1

One day his mother said
when Pierre climbed out of bed,

"Good morning, darling boy,
you are my only joy."
Pierre said, *"I don't care!"*
"What would you like to eat?"
"I don't care!"
"Some lovely cream of wheat?"
"I don't care!"
"Don't sit backwards on your chair."
"I don't care!"
"Or pour syrup on your hair."
"I don't care!"
"You are acting like a clown."
"I don't care!"
"And we have to go to town."
"I don't care!"
"Don't you want to come, my dear?"
"I don't care!"
"Would you rather stay right here?"
"I don't care!"
So his mother left him there.

CHAPTER 2

His father said, "Get off your head
or I will march you up to bed!"
Pierre said, *"I don't care!"*
"I would think that you could see—"
"I don't care!"
"Your head is where your feet should be!"
"I don't care!"

"If you keep standing upside down—"
"I don't care!"
"We'll never ever get to town."
"I don't care!"
"If only you would say I CARE."
"I don't care!"
"I'd let you fold the folding chair."
"I don't care!"

So his parents left him there.
They didn't take him anywhere.

CHAPTER 3

Now, as the night began to fall
a hungry lion paid a call.
He looked Pierre right in the eye
and asked him if he'd like to die.
Pierre said, *"I don't care!"*
"I can eat you, don't you see?"
"I don't care!"
"And you will be inside of me."
"I don't care!"
"Then you'll never have to bother—"
"I don't care!"
"With a mother and a father."
"I don't care!"
"Is that all you have to say?"
"I don't care!"
"Then I'll eat you, if I may."
"I don't care!"
So the lion ate Pierre.

CHAPTER 4

Arriving home at six o'clock,
his parents had a dreadful shock!
They found the lion sick in bed
and cried, "Pierre is surely dead!"
They pulled the lion by the hair.
They hit him with the folding chair.
His mother asked, "Where is Pierre?"
The lion answered, *"I don't care!"*
His father said, "Pierre's in there!"

CHAPTER 5

They rushed the lion into town.
The doctor shook him up and down.
And when the lion gave a roar—
Pierre fell out upon the floor.
He rubbed his eyes and scratched his head
and laughed because he wasn't dead.
His mother cried and held him tight.
His father asked, "Are you all right?"
Pierre said, "I am feeling fine,
please take me home, it's half past nine."
The lion said, "If you would care
to climb on me, I'll take you there."
Then everyone looked at Pierre who shouted,
"Yes, indeed I care!"
The lion took them home to rest
and stayed on as a weekend guest.
The moral of Pierre is CARE!

End of Act I

The stoop, a minute later. Pierre has now joined the other kids outside.

PIERRE   *(red-faced and shrieking)* So—what happened to Chicken Soup already?

ALL OF THEM   *(impatiently)* Yeah, Ro. What happened?

(Rosie whirls around. She does a bump and grind.)

ROSIE   Stop screaming! Stop yelling!

(The kids are delirious. They are finally going to hear what happened to Chicken Soup. All during Rosie's song, they dance and shout.)

SCREAMING AND YELLING

When everybody screams and yells,
Who calms them down?
Who rings their bells?
When everybody screams and yells,
The enchanted one
That's me.
When everybody screams and yells:
There's nothing to do! There's nothing to see!

Who dreams up a place they'd like to be?
The enchanted one
That's me.
It takes personality
A lot of personality
To make them see it my way.
It takes personality
More personality
To turn twelve boring hours
into a fascinating day!
I CAN DO IT!
That's a fact.
I CAN DO IT!
Don't you see?
AND I'LL DO IT
ALL FOR FREE!
Do you know?
Can you guess
who I simply have to be?
STOP SCREAMING AND YELLING AND
I'LL TELL YOU ALREADY!
The enchanted one
That's me.

(All the kids are seated on the stoop in front of Rosie. It is her great dramatic moment. There is a hushed silence.)

ROSIE   *(deep, ominous monotone)* Did you hear what happened to Chicken Soup?

(There is a clap of thunder. Rosie is more astonished than anyone. A deeper roll of thunder. All look up. The scene darkens, raindrops fall. The kids are motionless, caught in a fierce tension. Kathy spoils it all by whining.)

KATHY   I'm getting wet. I have to go in.

(The kids on the stoop stir nervously. Rosie feels her power oozing away; her big moment is about to be lost. The kids begin to stumble over each other, slowly, as in a dream. Buttermilk makes a dash for the backyard. This gives Rosie her cue.)

ROSIE   Quick, everybody! Follow me!

ALL OF THEM   *(voices overlapping)* I'm getting wet—big deal—go soak your head—oh shut up—stop shoving—I'm getting hungry—I don't care—etc.

(They follow Rosie into the backyard. The rain falls harder. Rosie pulls open the cellar door, and they all clamber down into the darkness. The door pounds shut after them. The kids sit around Rosie, panting, wet, and waiting. Thunder sounds different from inside. The raindrops on the cellar door sound like buckshot. Rosie is very excited. This setting is perfect for what follows; she couldn't have planned it better. She stares fixedly, slowly rises, and begins:)

THE BALLAD OF CHICKEN SOUP

Today our dear friend Chicken Soup,
this very ordinary day,
boiled up a pot of chicken soup
and swallowed it away.
A-lack! A-day!
O-woe! Oy-vay!
He swallowed it away!
Now listen to what I'm gonna say.
A little bone, a bitty thing
no bigger than my pinky—
he swallowed hot
from out that pot
in quicker than a winky.

He gulped that soup,
let out a whoop!
And fell down croaking
on the stoop.
And he CHOKED!
And he SAGGED!
And he SMOTHERED!
And he GAGGED!
And he let out a SCREAM!
And he let out a MOAN!
Then he cried
'cause he died
from choking on a bone
on such an ordinary day
like today.

KATHY   I can't believe it!

ALLIGATOR   Isn't it awful!

JOHNNY   I can't believe it! Tell us again!

PIERRE   Again! Again!

ALL OF THEM   Again! Again! Do it again, Rosie!

(Jennie barks noisily.)

ROSIE   Sure!

(Rosie sings a reprise. The kids join in as a croaking chorus.)

A-lack! A-day!

O-woe! Oy-vay!

On an ordinary day

Chicken Soup passed away!

(At the end of the song, they all lie sprawled out "dead" on the floor. The cellar door suddenly creaks open. A figure stands silhouetted against the light—it is Chicken Soup himself.)

CHICKEN SOUP   *(stepping over Rosie)* What are you all lying around for?

ALLIGATOR   We're dead!

CHICKEN SOUP   No kidding! I've been looking all over for you guys. Let's play something.

ROSIE   *(sits up and opens her arms wide)* Chicken Soup, sweetheart, I thought you'd never come!

(Everyone is shouting with excitement. Of course, no one seems to mind—or even notice—that Chicken Soup isn't dead. In the meantime, he dispenses paper cups filled with hot soup. All sip and murmur happily.)

ROSIE   You have to be in my movie!

CHICKEN SOUP   Sure. What do I have to do?

ROSIE   First, a screen test.

CHICKEN SOUP   O.K. I'll do "Chicken Soup With Rice"!

ALLIGATOR   Can I be in his screen test too?

ROSIE   Sure! Everybody can be in "Chicken Soup With Rice."

(They all laugh.)

ALL OF THEM   Hooray for Chicken Soup!

CHICKEN SOUP   Hooray for me!

ALL THE CHILDREN   Lights! Action! Camera!

("Chicken Soup With Rice," an elaborate production number a la Busby Berkeley, celebrates the seasons of the year, good food, and the business of living. The children take part with great gusto and joy, and when they are finished, they are tired —and hungry. It is nearly suppertime. Rosie definitely begins to lose them.)

CHICKEN SOUP WITH RICE

JANUARY

In January it's so nice
while slipping on the sliding ice
to sip hot chicken soup with rice.
Sipping once
sipping twice
sipping chicken soup with rice.

FEBRUARY

In February it will be
my snowman's anniversary
with cake for him and soup for me!
Happy once
happy twice
happy chicken soup with rice.

MARCH

In March the wind blows down the door
and spills my soup upon the floor.
It laps it up and roars for more.
Blowing once
blowing twice
blowing chicken soup with rice.

APRIL

In April I will go away
to far off Spain or old Bombay
and dream about hot soup all day.
Oh my oh once
oh my oh twice
oh my oh chicken soup with rice.

MAY

In May I truly think it best
to be a robin lightly dressed
concocting soup inside my nest.
Mix it once
mix it twice
mix that chicken soup with rice.

JUNE

In June I saw a charming group
of roses all begin to droop.
I pepped them up with chicken soup!
Sprinkle once
sprinkle twice
sprinkle chicken soup with rice.

JULY

In July I'll take a peep
into the cool and fishy deep
where chicken soup is selling cheap.
Selling once
selling twice
selling chicken soup with rice.

AUGUST

In August it will be so hot
I will become a cooking pot
cooking soup of course. Why not?
Cooking once
cooking twice
cooking chicken soup with rice.

SEPTEMBER

In September for a while
I will ride a crocodile
down the chicken soupy Nile.
Paddle once
paddle twice
paddle chicken soup with rice.

OCTOBER

In October I'll be host
to witches, goblins and a ghost.
I'll serve them chicken soup on toast.
Whoopy once
whoopy twice
whoopy chicken soup with rice.

NOVEMBER

In November's gusty gale
I will flop my flippy tail
and spout hot soup.
I'll be a whale!
Spouting once
spouting twice
spouting chicken soup with rice.

DECEMBER

In December I will be
a baubled bangled Christmas tree
with soup bowls draped all over me.
Merry once
merry twice
merry chicken soup with rice.

I told you once
I told you twice
all seasons of the year are nice
for eating chicken soup with rice!

ROSIE   O.K. You're all swell and you can all be in my picture!

   (Nobody is listening. Yawns and stretches.)

CHICKEN SOUP   I'm hungry!

   (Suddenly all the kids are leaving.)

ROSIE   *(nervously)* Let's get this show on the road!

(mournfully) Hey!

   (It is over. They are gone. She looks around, frustrated. Buttermilk is watching her. Rosie gently picks the cat up. She cuddles it and says:)

ROSIE   Wasn't that a swell movie?

BUTTERMILK   Meow.

ROSIE   You said it.

   It is twilight. Now Rosie is tired. She wanders out of the yard, singing the opening verses of "Really Rosie." We watch her from the back. At first her figure is somewhat dejected, but by the end of the song, she perks up. At the very last moment she looks at the evening sky and sees a star.

REALLY ROSIE

I'm really Rosie
And I'm Rosie Real.
You better believe me
I'm a great big deal!
BE-LIEVE ME!
I'm a star from afar,
Off the golden coast.
Beat that drum! Make that toast!
To Rosie the most!
BE-LIEVE ME!

The End

REALLY ROSIE

Lyrics by Maurice Sendak

Music by Carole King

ONE WAS JOHNNY

Lyrics by Maurice Sendak

Music by Carole King

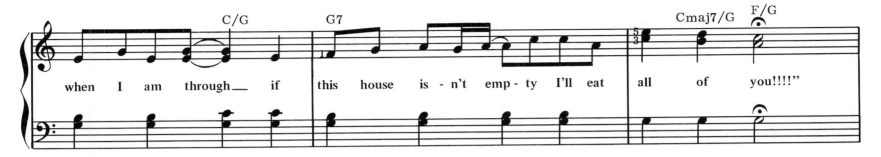

when I am through___ if this house is-n't emp-ty I'll eat all of you!!!!"

9 was the rob-ber who left___ look-ing pale   8 was the ti-ger who chased___ him to jail

Se-ven the black -bird flew off to Ha-va-na   6 was the mon-key who stole___ a ba-na-na

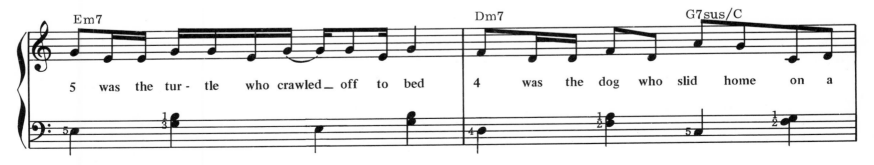

5 was the tur-tle who crawled___ off to bed   4 was the dog who slid home on a

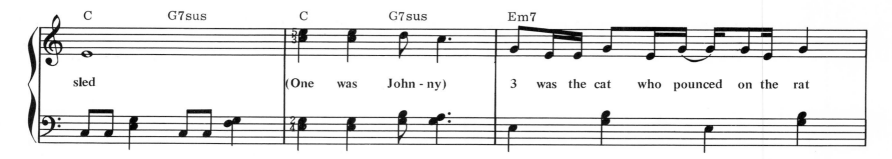

sled   (One was John - ny)   3 was the cat who pounced on the rat

2 was the rat who left— with the cat and—   1 was John - ny   (One was John - ny)

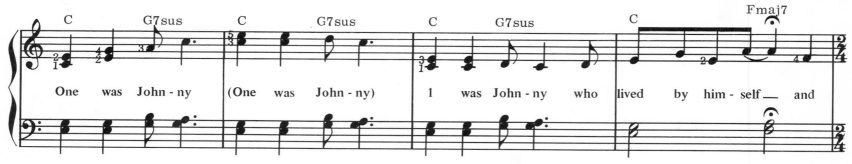

One was John - ny   (One was John - ny)   1 was John - ny who lived by him - self— and

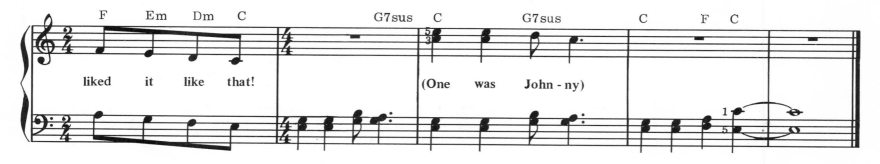

liked it like that!   (One was John - ny)

ALLIGATORS ALL AROUND

Lyrics by Maurice Sendak

Music by Carole King

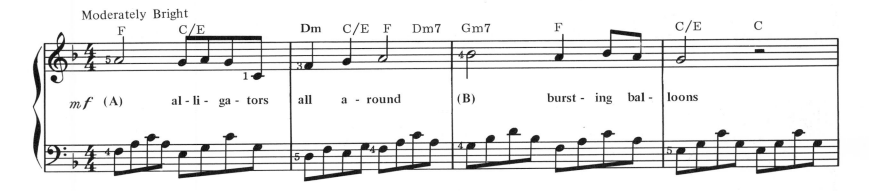

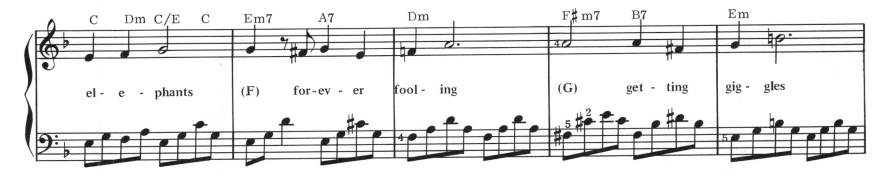

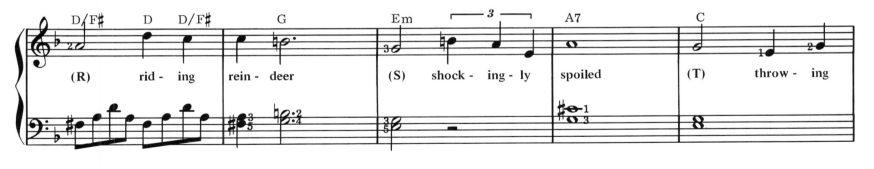

(R) rid - ing rein - deer (S) shock - ing - ly spoiled (T) throw - ing

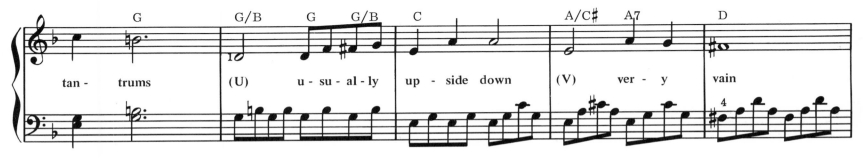

tan - trums (U) u - su - al - ly up - side down (V) ver - y vain

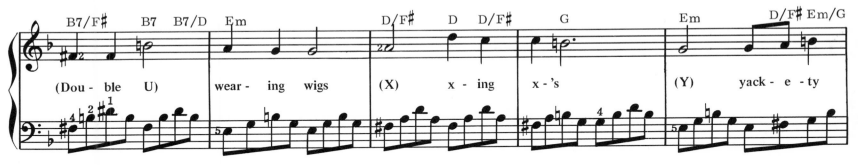

(Dou - ble U) wear - ing wigs (X) x - ing x - 's (Y) yack - e - ty

yack - ing (Z) Zip - pe - ty zound! (Zip - pe - ty zound)

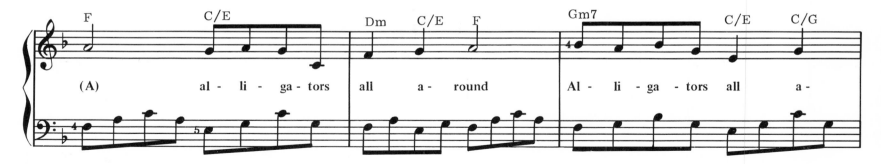

(A) al - li - ga - tors all a - round Al - li - ga - tors all a -

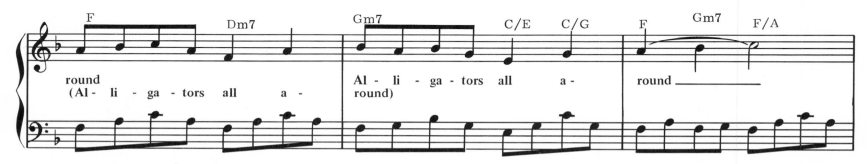

round Al - li - ga - tors all a - round

(Al - li - ga - tors all a - round)

Al - li - ga - tors all a - round Al - li - ga - tors all a -

round (Al - li - ga - tors all a - round)

round.

PIERRE

Lyrics by Maurice Sendak

Music by Carole King

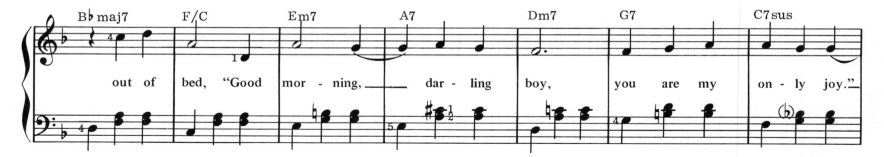

Bb maj7 · F/C · Em7 · A7 · Dm7 · G7 · C7sus

out of   bed, "Good   mor - ning,____ dar - ling   boy,   you   are   my   on - ly joy."

Gm7 · C7 · Fmaj7 · Bb maj7 · Fmaj7 · Em7 · A7

____ Pi -   erre ____ said, ____   "I   don't   care!"

Dm · A7/C# · Dm · A7/C#

"What   would   you   like   to   eat?"   "I   don't   care!"   "Some   love - ly   cream   of   wheat?"   " I   don't

Bb maj7 · C7sus/F · F · Bb maj7 · C7sus/F

care!"   "Don't   sit   back - wards   on   your chair."   "I   don't   care!"   "Or   pour   syr - up   on

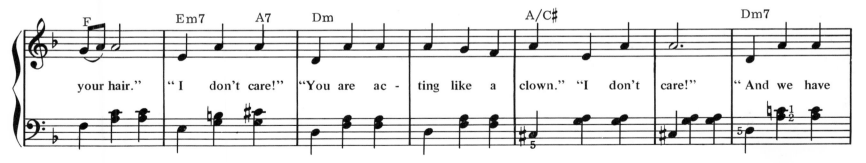

F   Em7   A7   Dm   A/C♯   Dm7

your hair."   "I   don't care!"   "You are ac - ting like a   clown." "I   don't   care!"   "And we have

G7   Gm7   C7sus/F   Fmaj7

to   go to   town." "I   don't   care!"   "Don't you   want   to come,   my dear?" "I   don't care!"

B♭maj7   C7sus/F   F   Dm7   G7   Dm7

"Would you   ra - ther stay   right here?" "I   don't   care!" So   his   mo -   ther

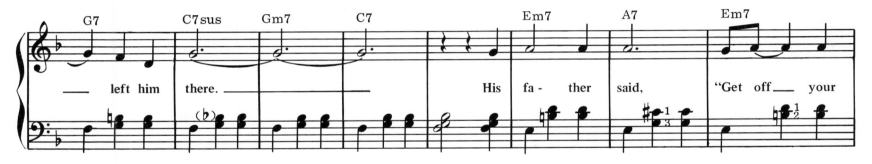

G7   C7sus   Gm7   C7   Em7   A7   Em7

left him   there.   His   fa - ther   said,   "Get off   your

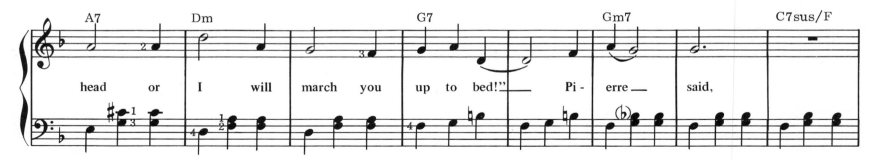

head   or   I   will   march   you   up to bed!"—   Pi-   erre—   said,

"I   don't   care!"   "I   would   think   that   you   could   see—"   "I
                                        "I   can   eat   you,   don't   you   see?"   "I

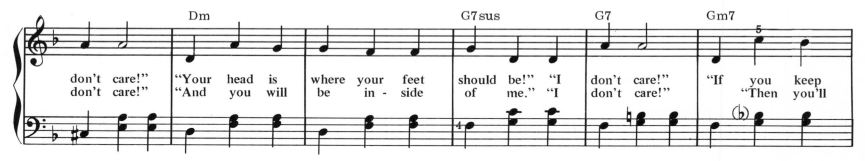

don't care!"   "Your   head   is   where   your   feet   should   be!"   "I   don't   care!"   "If   you   keep
don't care!"   "And   you   will   be   in-   side   of   me."   "I   don't   care!"   "Then   you'll

stan-   ding   up-   side—   down—"   "I   don't   care!"   "We'll   ne-   ver   e-   ver   get   to—   town"
ne-   ver   have   to—   bo-   ther—"   "I   don't   care!"   "With   a   mo-   ther   and   a—   fa-   ther."

Em7   A7   Dm   A/C#

"I don't care!" "If on - ly you would say I care." "I don't care!"
"I don't care!" "Is that all you have to say?" "I don't care!"

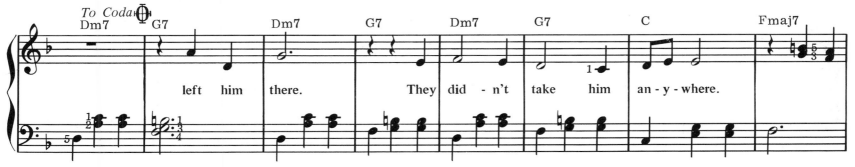

Dm   G7sus   Dm7   G7

"I'd let you fold the fol - ding chair." "I don't care!" So his par - ents
"Then I'll eat you, if I may." "I don't care!" So the li - on

To Coda Dm7   G7   Dm7   G7   Dm7   G7   C   Fmaj7

left him there. They did - n't take him an - y - where.

Cmaj7   Fmaj7   Cmaj7   Fmaj7   Cmaj7   Am

Now, as the night be -

47

gan__ to fall a hun - gry li - on paid __ a call. He looked Pi - erre ____

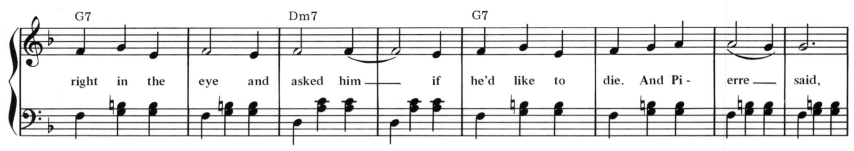

right in the eye and asked him ____ if he'd like to die. And Pi - erre ___ said,

D.S. al Coda

"I don't care!"

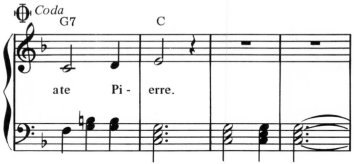

Coda

ate Pi - erre.

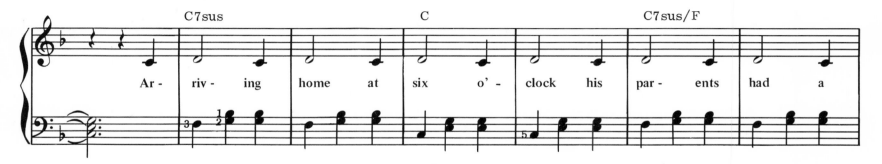

Ar - riv - ing home at six o' - clock his par - ents had a

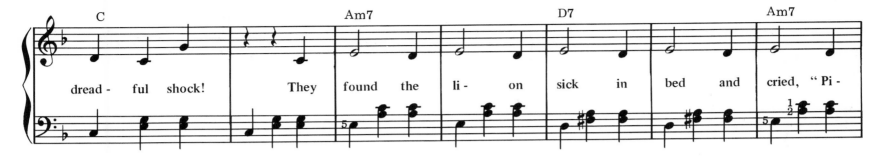

dread - ful shock! They found the li - on sick in bed and cried, " Pi -

erre is sure - ly dead!" They pulled the li - on by the hair. They hit him

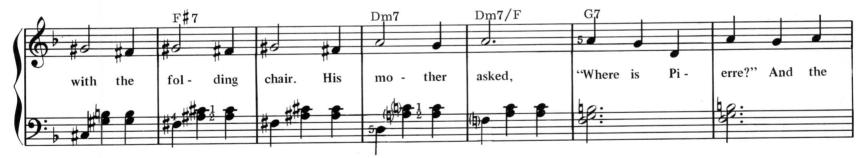

with the fol - ding chair. His mo - ther asked, "Where is Pi - erre?" And the

li - on an - swered, ____ " I don't care!" His

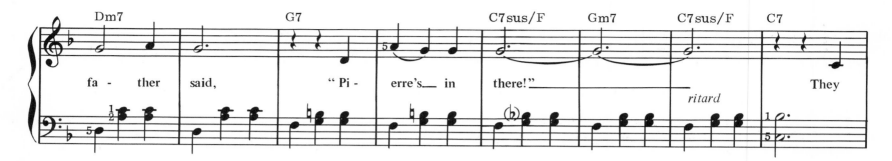

fa - ther said, "Pi - erre's__ in there!"_____ *ritard* They

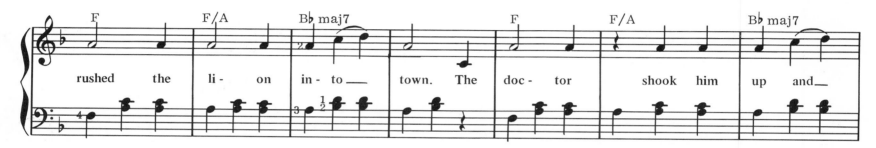

rushed the li - on in - to __ town. The doc - tor shook him up and__

down. And when the li - on gave a roar— Pi - erre fell out

up - on the floor._____ He rubbed his eyes and

50

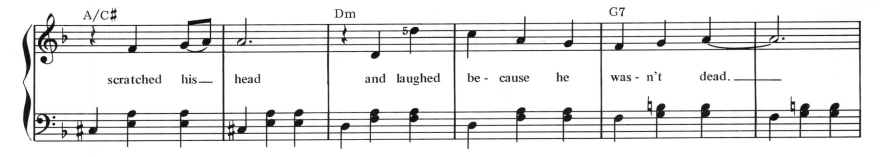

scratched his — head   and laughed   be - cause he   was - n't   dead. —

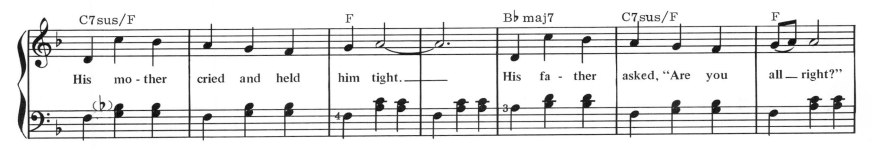

His mo - ther   cried and held   him tight. —   His fa - ther   asked, "Are you   all — right?"

Pi - erre said,   "I am feel -   ing — fine,   please —   take   me   home, it's half

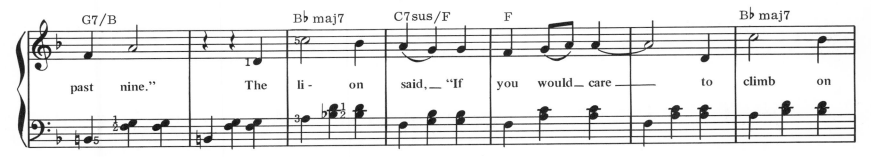

past   nine."   The li -   on said, — "If   you would — care —   to climb   on

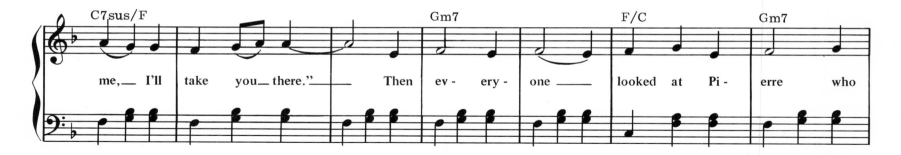

C7sus/F ... Gm7 ... F/C ... Gm7

me,__ I'll take you__ there." __ Then ev-ery-one __ looked at Pi - erre who

Fmaj7 ... B♭maj7 ... Gm7 ... C7sus/F

shou - ted, "Yes in - deed I __ care!" The li - on took them home to rest and

F ... Dm7 ... Gm7 ... C7sus ... C7

stayed on __ as a week - end __ guest. The mor - al of Pi - erre is

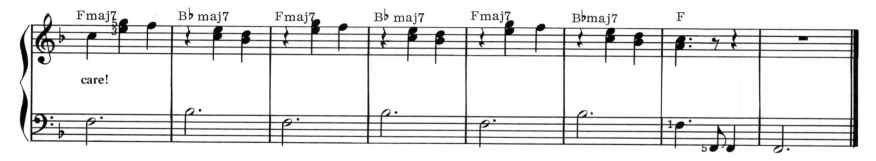

Fmaj7 ... B♭maj7 ... Fmaj7 ... B♭maj7 ... Fmaj7 ... B♭maj7 ... F

care!

SCREAMING AND YELLING

Lyrics by Maurice Sendak

Music by Carole King

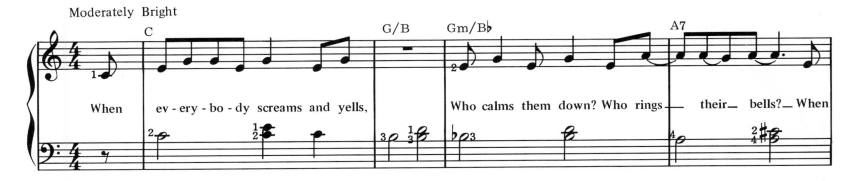

When ev-ery-bo-dy screams and yells, Who calms them down? Who rings their bells? When

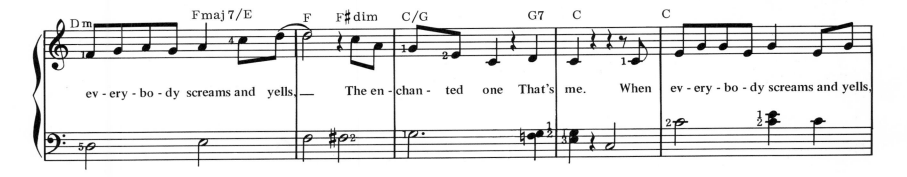

ev-ery-bo-dy screams and yells,— The en-chan-ted one That's me. When ev-ery-bo-dy screams and yells,

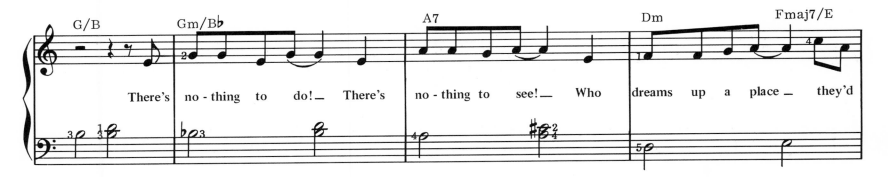

There's no-thing to do!— There's no-thing to see!— Who dreams up a place— they'd

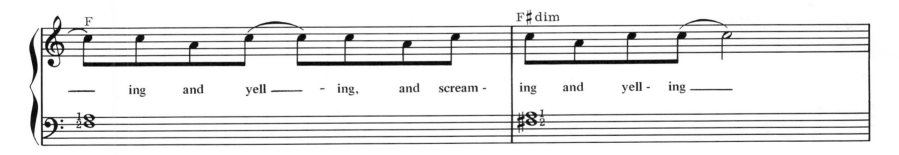

THE BALLAD OF CHICKEN SOUP

Lyrics by Maurice Sendak

Music by Carole King

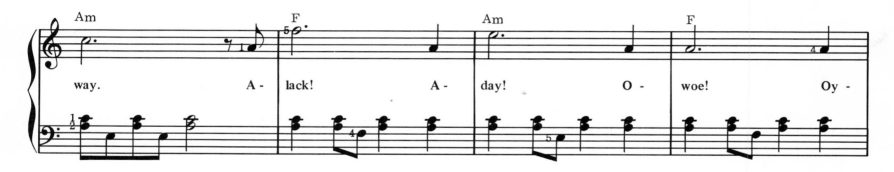

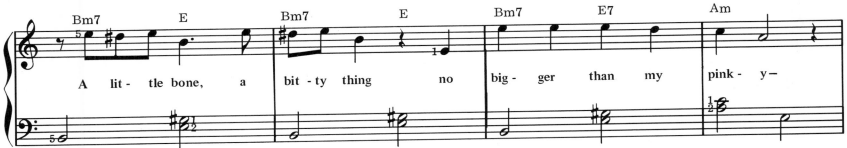

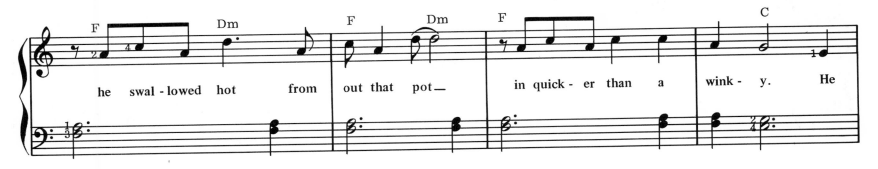

on— the stoop. And he choked!— Agh! And he sagged! And he smo - thered! And he

gagged! And he let out a scream! Aagh! And he let out a moan!—

Oh! Then he cried 'cause he died from cho - king on a bone—

on such an or - di - nar - y— day like to - day.

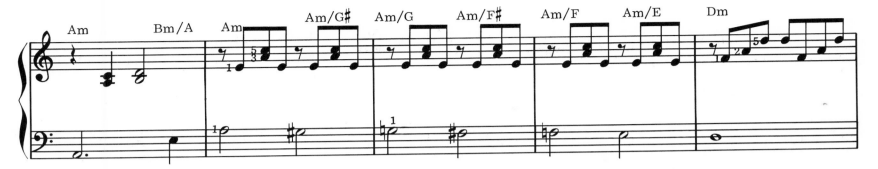

A - lack! A -

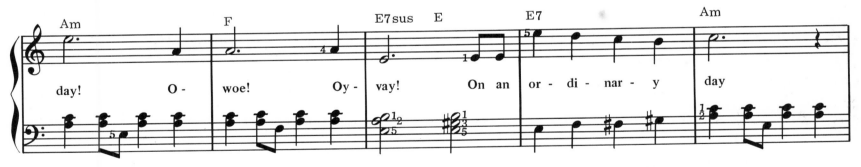

day! O - woe! Oy - vay! On an or - di - nar - y day

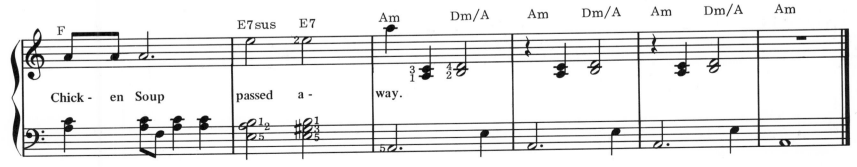

Chick - en Soup passed a - way.

CHICKEN SOUP WITH RICE

Lyrics by Maurice Sendak

Music by Carole King

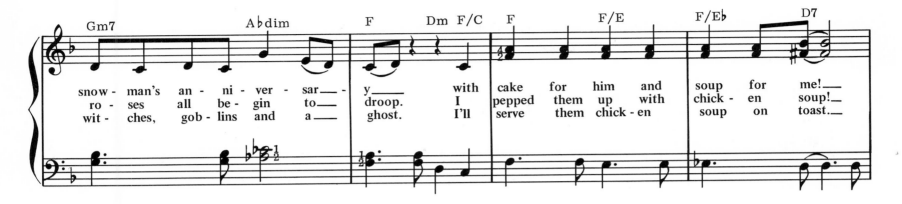

Gm7 ... A♭dim ... F ... Dm F/C ... F ... F/E ... F/E♭ ... D7

snow - man's an - ni - ver - sar - y droop. with cake for him and soup for me!
ro - ses all be - gin to - droop. I pepped them up with chick - en soup!
wit - ches, gob - lins and a - ghost. I'll serve them chick - en soup on toast.

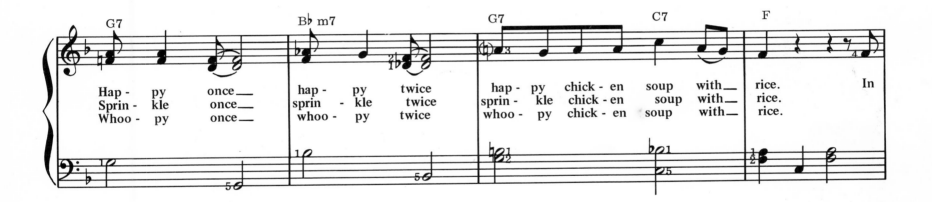

G7 ... B♭m7 ... G7 ... C7 ... F

Hap - py once hap - py twice hap - py chick - en soup with rice.
Sprin - kle once sprin - kle twice sprin - kle chick - en soup with rice.
Whoo - py once whoo - py twice whoo - py chick - en soup with rice.

In

Cm7 ... F7 ... B♭ ... Cm7 ... B♭/D Cm7 B♭

March the wind blows down the door and spills my soup up - on the floor. It
In Ju - ly I'll take a peep and in - to my cool and fish - y deep where
In No - vem - ber's gus - ty gale I will flop my flip - py tail and

61

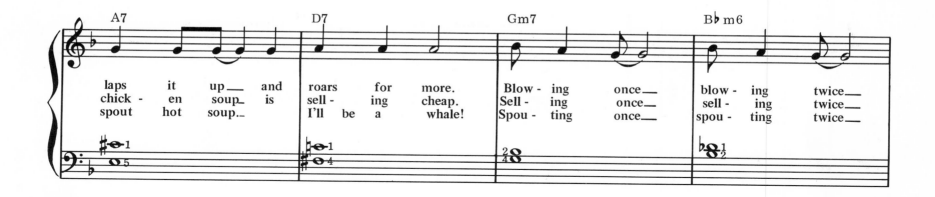

laps   it   up__ and   roars   for   more.
chick - en   soup__ is   sell - ing   cheap.
spout   hot   soup..   I'll   be   a   whale!

Blow - ing   once__   blow - ing   twice__
Sell - ing   once__   sell - ing   twice__
Spou - ting   once__   spou - ting   twice__

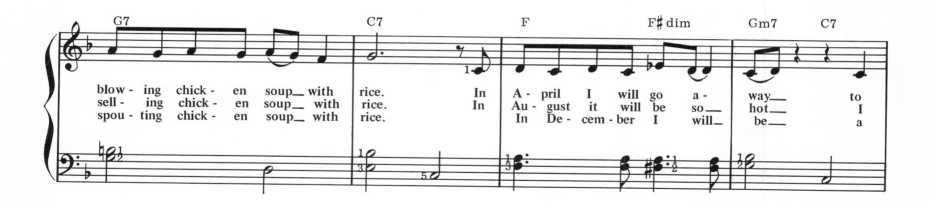

blow - ing   chick - en   soup__ with   rice.   In
sell - ing   chick - en   soup__ with   rice.   In
spou - ting   chick - en   soup__ with   rice.   In

A - pril   I   will   go   a -   way__   to
Au - gust   it   will   be   so   hot__   I
De - cem - ber   I   will__   be__   a

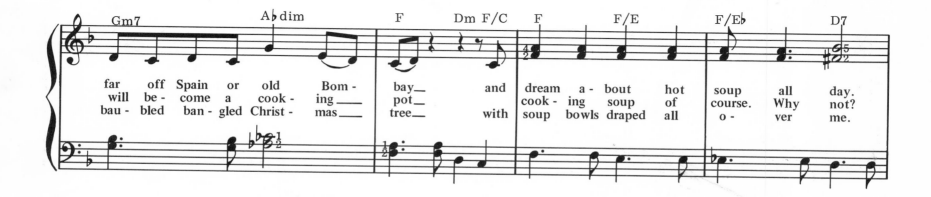

far   off   Spain   or   old   Bom -   bay__   and
will   be - come   a   cook - ing ____   pot__   with
bau - bled   ban - gled   Christ - mas ____   tree__

dream   a - bout   hot   soup   all   day.
cook - ing   soup   of   course.   Why   not?
soup   bowls   draped   all   o -   ver   me.

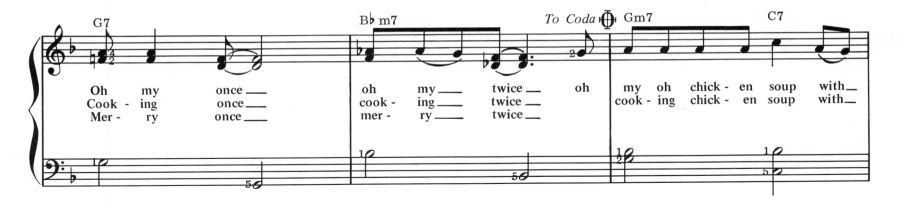